# Curse of The Pharaoh's Treasure

N. A. Seidel

*This book is dedicated to all the dreamers, explorers, and storytellers. With every page, we venture into the unknown—places where myths live, mysteries unravel, and the impossible becomes reality. These short stories are just the beginning of countless adventures that lie ahead. May this series ignite your imagination and take you to lands you've never seen before. Here's to many more tales that inspire, thrill, and transport us to worlds we've only dreamed of – N. A. Seidel*

# CONTENTS

# PROLOGUE

## KING TUTANKHAMUN

In the heart of ancient Egypt, where the scorching sunbathed the desert sands in gold, legends of the Pharaoh's treasures whispered through the ages. Among them, none were more feared than the treasure of Tutankhamun, the boy king whose wealth was said to be guarded by the gods themselves.

Buried deep beneath the shifting dunes, his tomb remained untouched for centuries, protected by curses, traps, and the relentless vigilance of the gods.

Those who dared seek the treasure often vanished without a trace, their fates sealed by the ancient deities who watched over the Pharaoh's resting place. Some said it was the wrath of Anubis, the god of death, while others believed Ra, the sun god, blinded those who trespassed.

But one thing was certain—once disturbed, the treasure of Tutankhamun unleashed a curse that could not be undone.

Now, centuries later, as the world moves forward

and modern civilization forgets the old gods, three young adventurers unknowingly enter a mystery far beyond their understanding.

Eli, Karly, and Nathan, on what was supposed to be a simple school trip to Cairo, find themselves caught in the snare of an ancient curse. What begins as a fascination with a dusty old tablet soon unravels into a deadly quest through forgotten tombs, puzzles of the gods, and a treasure guarded by the divine.

The past is alive, and some secrets are never meant to be uncovered.

# CHAPTER 1

## SCHOOL TRIP TO EGYPT

Egypt was hot, not just regular summer hot, but the kind of heat that clung to you like a heavy blanket. The relentless and bright sun hung in the vast, cloudless sky, casting golden rays over the busy streets of Cairo.

Tourists poured out of buses, fanning their faces, clutching water bottles, and snapping pictures of anything that remotely looked ancient. It was a world entirely different from the suburban school life Eli, Karly, and Nathan were used to.

The trio shuffled behind the rest of their class, trailing through the streets toward the Cairo Museum of Antiquities. Eli's backpack nearly dragged on the ground as he groaned,

"Why did I pack so much?".

Karly was ahead of him, practically bouncing with excitement, and Nathan was somewhere in the middle, keeping an eye out for anything interesting enough to distract his attention from the constant chatter of their tour guide, Mr. Duncan.

"Come on, Eli! We're in Egypt! You have to pretend at least you're enjoying this!" Karly called, throwing an encouraging look over her shoulder. "I am," Eli grumbled, kicking a loose stone down the sidewalk. "Just not sure I signed up to listen to Mr. Duncan's hour-long lectures every ten minutes. Does he ever stop talking?" Karly shot him a grin.

"Could be worse. You could've been stuck with Ms. Donahue's history lesson instead." Eli let out another groan. "Don't remind me," Nathan smirked from his position just ahead of Eli. "Hey, at least Duncan knows his stuff. Besides, how often do you walk through an actual pyramid?" "That's next week," Karly reminded them. "We're doing the museum today."

"Oh great," Nathan said, his voice dripping with sarcasm. "More dusty artifacts." "It's not just dusty artifacts. It's Tutankhamun's treasure. Have some respect for ancient history, Nathan!" Karly replied. Eli stifled a laugh. Typical Karly.

Always the one obsessed with history, always

ready to jump into anything mysterious or old. On the other hand, Nathan is always looking for the next thrill, and Eli just wanted to survive the heat.

The cool air felt like stepping into another world as they entered the museum. The noise of the outside city faded, replaced by the quiet whispers of tourists and the steady hum of the air conditioning. Glass cases filled with golden artifacts, ancient pottery, and dusty papyrus scrolls lined the halls. It was overwhelming how much history was crammed into one place.

"Alright, students," Mr. Duncan announced, his voice far too excited for the early hour. "We'll start with the exhibits on the Pharaohs of the New Kingdom. Make sure you stay close and don't touch anything."

The students groaned but followed closely. Nathan walked up to Eli, a mischievous grin spreading across his face. "Bet you twenty bucks we find something cursed in here or something magical," Nathan said in a low voice.

Eli shot him a side glance. "You've been watching too many movies." "Or not enough," Nathan replied with a wink. "I mean, come on, we're in a place filled with ancient Egyptian treasures. There's gotta be some spooky stuff." Karly, walking ahead of them, turned back. "Actually, there are a lot of curses in Egyptian history, mostly associated with tombs and treasures. Pharaohs used them to protect their belongings in the afterlife."

Nathan's smiled excitedly, poking Eli in the ribs, "See? Cursed treasure. I told you." "That doesn't mean we're going to find anything cursed here," Eli pointed out. "You never know," Nathan said, looking at the rows of artifacts like he was ready to spot something suspicious at any moment.

The group stopped in front of a massive glass case, inside of which lay a pristine golden mask— Tutankhamun's funeral mask. It gleamed under the museum lights, every intricate detail shimmering with the allure of ancient royalty.

"It's amazing; look at how majestic it is," Karly said, staring at its beauty. Nathan whistled low. "Man, I wouldn't mind having that in my room. Wouldn't that freak out your little brother, Eli?" "Sure," Eli replied, still distracted by the museum's size and beauty. His eyes wandered past the group and settled on a dimly lit corner of the hall, where fewer tourists gathered.

There, at the edge of the exhibit, was a smaller display. It wasn't grand or flashy, unlike the golden artifacts in the rest of the museum. It looked as if the museum staff had forgotten it was even there. Dust clung to the glass, and a flickering light overhead cast faint shadows on the display. Inside the case lay a cracked stone tablet etched with strange symbols and lines. It was old, ancient even, but something roused Eli's curiosity. He squinted, trying to make out the symbols.

"Hey, guys... check this out," Eli called, waving Karly and Nathan over. They approached cautiously, looking at the artifact Eli was pointing at. "What is this, I wonder?" Karly asked out loud.

"Looks like a treasure map to me," Nathan said, trying to get a closer look. "It's not a treasure map," Karly countered, rolling her eyes. "It's just some ancient writing." Nathan shrugged his shoulders. "Looks like a map to me."

Eli leaned in closer, his face nearly pressed to the glass. He wasn't sure if it was the flickering light or something else, but the lines on the stone tablet seemed to shimmer as if they were moving, rearranging themselves in his mind. He blinked, and suddenly, the symbols looked clearer, almost as if they made sense now.

"It does look like a map," Eli muttered suddenly. "See? Told you," Nathan replied, shooting a look at Karly. "But why would there be a map in the middle of an exhibit like this? It doesn't make any sense. This doesn't belong here," she replied. "I agree," Eli replied, but something about the tablet kept drawing him in. It felt important. He couldn't explain why, but something about it pulled at him in a way nothing else in the museum had.

Mr. Duncan's voice broke through their quiet discussion. "Alright, students, gather around. We're moving to the next exhibit." Eli stayed frozen in front of the glass case. He wasn't ready to leave yet. The tablet seemed to call to him, pulling him in like a magnet.

"You coming or what man?" Nathan asked as he walked away. "Eli!" Karly said in a raised whisper, throwing her hands up in the air. "Come on!" A museum attendant shot her a look, causing Karly to walk off with the group quickly.

Reluctantly, he stepped away from the case, but not before his eyes caught one last glimpse of the shimmering symbols. The image of the lines burned in his mind, and even as they moved on to the next exhibit, he couldn't shake the feeling that the tablet was more than just a dusty old artifact.

Later that night, back at their hotel, the three had gathered in Nathan's room, sprawled out on the bed and floor, the tablet fresh in their minds. "Okay, let's think about this," Nathan said, tapping a pen against a notepad. "We saw what looked like a treasure map in the middle of a museum filled with priceless artifacts." Karly shook her head. "It's not a treasure map. It's probably some ancient navigation tool or something. You guys are making this into more than it is."

"But what if it is?" Nathan replied, leaning forward. "I mean, it's not like it's impossible. There have been stories of buried treasure all over Egypt. Didn't you ever watch any of those mummy movies?" Eli stayed quiet, still thinking about the shimmering lines he had seen on the tablet.

It felt impossible, but he couldn't shake the feeling that they were on to something. Something big.

"Even if it was a treasure map, what are we supposed to do? We're on a school trip. It's not like we can just sneak out and start looking for ancient treasure," said Karly. Nathan's expression changed almost immediately as he jumped up in joy.

"Why not? Why can't we have a little adventure!?" Nathan asked, grinning. "Where's your sense of adventure?" Karly crossed her arms. "I'd rather not get cursed, thanks or even worse, kicked out of school."

Nathan scoffed. "Curses aren't real. They're just stories people made up to scare treasure hunters away." "I'm not sure about that," Eli replied. The room fell into silence as the three of them thought it through. It was one thing to joke about curses and treasure maps, but it was another to consider the possibility that they were real.

Nathan clapped his hands. "Alright, here's what we do: tomorrow, we sneak out of the tour and head back to the museum. We take another look at that tablet and see if we can figure out where it leads." Karly looked at him like he'd lost his mind. "Are you serious? That's a terrible idea that might get us sent home," Karly replied. Nathan shrugged. "Terrible, maybe. But exciting? Definitely."

Eli was excited at the thought of sneaking back into the museum, but a part of him was curious, too. What if they had stumbled onto something bigger than they realized?

What if the tablet did lead to a hidden treasure, something buried deep beneath the sands of Egypt, untouched for thousands of years? "Eli?" Karly's voice snapped him out of his thoughts. "You're not seriously considering this, are you?"

Eli's mind was going at a million miles an hour. It was risky. It was dangerous. But there was something about the ancient and mysterious tablet that called to him in a way he couldn't ignore. "I don't know," Eli said finally. "But I think we should check it out." Nathan grinned triumphantly while Karly groaned in disapproval.

"You guys are going to get us all expelled," she muttered, but there was a hint of excitement in her voice. Eli's mind buzzed with a growing unease as the hours ticked and their plan slowly took shape. The excitement from earlier had dimmed, replaced by a gnawing sense that they were heading toward something far beyond their understanding—something bigger, darker, and far more dangerous than any of them were prepared for.

Whatever they had stumbled upon in that forgotten museum corner wasn't just an ordinary artifact. It was connected to something ancient that had been hidden for a reason.

The thought sent a shiver down his body despite the night's warmth. Every instinct told him to walk away, to let the map stay buried in the past where it belonged.

Yet, as he lay back in silence, the image of the tablet's symbols crept into his mind again. They pulsed faintly in his memory, the lines shifting as if they were alive, observing him. It was as though the symbols themselves were waiting patiently for the three to make their choice. There was a lingering presence in those ancient etchings, watching from the shadows, waiting to see if they would unlock a mystery that should have remained sealed.

# CHAPTER 2

## MUSEUM MADNESS

Eli shoved Nathan hard in the ribs, waking him. "What is, what's going on?" Nathan said sleepily. "Get up; we're going to get Karly and go back to the museum right now", Eli replied. "Really, did you have to be so rough?" Nathan replied, still confused as to what was happening.

"Yes, get up; we will grab Karly on the way out", he replied. Nathan stumbled out of bed and pulled on a pair of jeans and shoes. The pair left the hotel room they were staying in.

Eli pulled his phone out and called Karly. Nathan could hear her voice. "Hey, everything okay?" she replied. "Let's go," he replied before hanging up. "You two planned this without me!?" Nathan whispered loudly to Eli. He laughed as the three of them left the hotel.

The streets of Cairo were far from quiet, even late at night. The distant hum of the bustling city mixed with the occasional honking of cars, and faint conversations drifted on the breeze as people went about their lives. But the city was a blur for Eli, Karly, and Nathan. Their minds were locked on one thing— the museum.

The three had been restless since they'd left the Cairo Museum of Antiquities earlier that day. The golden treasures and ancient relics were impressive, but nothing compared to the stone tablet they had found in the far corner of the museum. Its cracked surface, etched with strange symbols, seemed to promise a secret—one that none of them could let go.

Eli shifted his weight as they crouched behind a tall stone wall on the outskirts of the museum's courtyard. The museum's towering structure loomed ahead, dark and quiet except for the occasional beam of light from the security guards making their rounds.

"Are you sure about this?" Eli whispered. "I mean, breaking into a museum at night? We could get into serious trouble." Karly gave him a glance, her eyes gleaming with adventure. "It's not breaking in if we were already there earlier, right? We're just returning."

"Yeah, sure," Eli said. "Returning in the middle of the night, past closing hours. No big deal." Nathan flashed them both a grin as he crouched beside them, pulling his phone out from his pocket. "Come on, Eli, don't be such a downer. How often do you get to sneak into a museum at night in a place like Egypt? This is the stuff movies are made of."

Eli couldn't argue with that. There was a strange thrill in what they were about to do, even if his nerves were buzzing. He cast a glance up at the museum again.

The grand entrance was locked tight, but the side door, the one the staff used, was their target. They had scoped it out earlier during the day, and Karly pointed out that it seemed less guarded than the front.

"You sure the security cameras don't catch this corner?" Nathan asked as he checked his phone for the time and then looked around cautiously. "I've been paying attention. The cameras are aimed more toward the exhibits, not the staff entrance.

We just need to be quick," Karly replied. Eli took a deep breath. Cairo at night was different from what he had imagined. During the day, the city felt alive, the streets buzzing with energy and excitement. But now, the dim lights of distant shops and the quiet shadows of ancient buildings gave the city a mysterious edge.

Even the desert beyond the city seemed to crawl with mystery, its vast emptiness filled with secrets. The pyramids they'd visited earlier in the week were only a short drive away. Thinking about those massive structures, standing silent and ancient in the night, made Eli shiver. "Alright," Nathan whispered.

"Let's do this." Without another word, the three slipped along the courtyard's edge, sticking to the shadows the tall stone walls cast. Their footsteps were muffled by the soft sand beneath their shoes as they approached the staff entrance.

Karly reached the door first. She tugged on the handle, testing it gently. It didn't budge. Maybe this was a sign that they shouldn't do this after all. But then, with a soft click, Karly produced a small tool tucked into her jacket pocket and began working at the lock.

"Where did you even learn to do that?" Eli asked, his voice tinged with both admiration and worry. "You'd be surprised what you can learn online," she replied.

A few seconds later, the door swung open just wide enough for them to slip inside. Compared to the warm night outside, the air in the museum was cool and dry.

The faint smell of old stone and ancient artifacts clung to the air, and the dim emergency lights cast long shadows across the marble floors. The Cairo Museum was unlike anything back home; it wasn't just a place for learning.

It was a house of history. The relics here were thousands of years old, and somewhere in its depths was the tablet that had captured their curiosity earlier that day.

Nathan flicked on his flashlight, its beam cutting through the dimness as they navigated the narrow hallways. Karly pulled out her phone, the screen glowing faintly as she used it to check their path. "We'll head straight for the Ancient Egypt wing," she whispered. That's where we found the tablet." The hallways stretched ahead of them, and the museum's quietness was almost eerie.

Eli glanced around nervously, half-expecting to see the stone eyes of a statue following their movements. They moved quickly, the only sounds were the soft padding of their shoes on the floor and the distant noise of the museum's air system. The walls were lined with ancient Egyptian paintings, and even in the dim light, the figures of gods and pharaohs seemed to glow with an otherworldly energy.

"Are we going to figure this out?" Eli asked quietly as they approached the entrance to the Egyptian wing. "I mean, we're just kids. We've never done anything like this before." "That's what makes it exciting," Nathan replied, his grin barely visible in the dark museum.

"Besides, if that tablet really is a map, then we're on the edge of something huge. Imagine what we could find." Karly's eyes sparkled with excitement as they reached the door to the room where the tablet was displayed. She pushed it open gently, and they slipped inside.

The room was dark, but the faint outlines of the artifacts were visible in the shadows. The tablet, still resting in its glass case in the far corner, seemed to call to them.

The cracked stone surface gleamed faintly under the emergency lights, the symbols etched into its surface more mysterious than ever. Karly hurried over, pulled out her phone, and began snapping pictures of the tablet. "Alright, let's see what we can figure out," she said.

Nathan joined her, his flashlight sweeping over the tablet as they examined the symbols more closely. Eli hung back, feeling concerned about what they were doing.

There was something about this place, about this moment, that felt different, like they were trespassing on something they shouldn't be touching. "Look at this," Karly said to Eli and Nathan. She held up her phone, the screen showing a close-up of one of the symbols on the tablet. "I think this one represents Ra, the sun god. And this one could be Horus."

"How do you know?" Nathan snapped. "I've been reading about it since we got here," Karly explained. "These gods were often used to mark sacred places or treasures. This could be a key to understanding the rest of the map."

Nathan pulled out his phone and opened an app that could scan and translate Egyptian hieroglyphs. "Let's see if this app can help us. It's not perfect, but it might give us a clue."

As they worked together, the symbols on the tablet began to make more sense. They weren't just random markings, they formed a series of clues, hints pointing toward something hidden along the

Nile River. "Look," Karly said, her voice filled with excitement. "This part here talks about a hidden chamber beneath the river. Something tied to Tutankhamun. It says... 'where the sun and river meet, the pharaoh's treasures shall sleep."

This was more than they had bargained for. The Treasure of Tutankhamun? That was the stuff of legend, untouched and unseen for thousands of years. Nathan pointed to another part of the inscription.

"And this part mentions 'a trial of the gods'." Karly leaned in for a closer look. "It's a warning. The gods have set trials to protect the treasure. We'll need to solve them if we're going to find it." This wasn't just some ancient map leading to treasure. It was something much bigger, something sacred and dangerous.

A strange whisper ran through the room briefly as the three looked up, startled. "Do you guys feel that?" Nathan asked. Eli swallowed, clearing his throat quietly. "Yeah, it's like... the air just got a bit more ancient." "It's probably just the ventilation system," Karly replied. The silence seemed to deepen, and a faint flickering light danced at the edges of their vision.

Suddenly, the lights overhead flickered, just

once, then twice, and the shadows in the room seemed to stretch and twist unnaturally. A faint whispering sound drifted through the air again, low and soft, as if carried on a breeze that didn't exist.

"What was that?" Nathan whispered as he stared at the door. The whispering grew louder, words forming in a language none could understand. The symbols on the tablet seemed to glow faintly, pulsing in time with the whispers.

"We need to get out of here," Eli said firmly, looking at Nathan. But before any of them could move, the unmistakable sound of footsteps echoed through the hallway outside the room. Steady, deliberate footsteps. Someone—or something—was coming.

Without a second thought, the three grabbed the tablet and left the museum quickly without being seen. Nothing was said as they all returned to the hotel for some well earned sleep.

# CHAPTER 3

## THE NILE CRUISE

The sun rose lazily over the horizon, casting a warm golden glow across the city of Cairo. The air was already thick with heat, promising another sweltering day in Egypt.

The school group had gathered early that morning, bags packed and sunglasses on, ready for a calm, scenic day along the legendary Nile River. But for Eli, Karly, and Nathan, the excitement from last night's adventure still buzzed under the surface. Nathan squinted through tired eyes.

They boarded the large, white riverboat with the rest of their classmates, chatter and laughter filling the air. Their teacher, Mr. Duncan, was at the front of the group, talking animatedly about the importance of the Nile throughout Egyptian history.

His words were hard to hear over the noise of the boat's engines starting up. The three, however, weren't listening.

Eli looked at the riverbank, which stretched far into the distance, while Karly clutched her phone tightly, her fingers itching to pull out the pictures she had taken of the tablet the night before. Nathan, as usual, leaned against the railing, eyes scanning the river as if expecting something to rise out of the water at any moment.

"Can you believe it?" Nathan said excitedly, glancing sideways at Eli and Karly. "We're cruising down the same river the Pharaohs once sailed on. And that map pointed to something along here. This is it. We're right where we need to be."

Karly pulled up the image of the tablet on her phone. Her eyes lit up with excitement. "The symbols on the map keep leading us toward the Nile. It must point to something hidden beneath the river or along the banks."

Eli shifted uncomfortably, still unsure how he felt about all of this. Last night had felt surreal—the museum, the strange symbols glowing on the tablet, the footsteps in the dark hallway. "I don't know, guys," Eli said, keeping his voice low. "What if this is something we're not supposed to find? We're just kids messing around with ancient Egyptian secrets."

"Come on, Eli," Nathan said, grinning. "You weren't complaining last night when we were decoding those hieroglyphs. Don't tell me you're chickening out now."

Eli sighed, glancing over at the vast expanse of water stretching out before them. The Nile River was breathtaking, shimmering under the morning sun. Palm trees lined the banks, their green leaves swaying gently in the breeze.

The river itself looked calm and peaceful, flowing steadily as it had for thousands of years. But beneath that calm surface, Eli felt that something else lay hidden. Something old, something powerful.

As the boat pushed away from the dock, the trio retreated to the back deck, away from the rest of the group.

The soft rumble of the boat's engines filled the air as it drifted further down the river, passing small villages, ancient ruins, and patches of green farmland nestled along the banks.

Karly pulled out a small notebook she had packed for the trip and flipped it open. "Okay, so based on what we figured out last night, the part of the map that mentions 'where the sun and river meet' must be talking about somewhere along the Nile. If we can match the landmarks we pass with the hieroglyphs, we might be able to narrow down the location." "But this river goes on forever. How are we supposed to know where to start looking?" Eli asked curiously.

Karly tapped her phone, pulling up the picture of the tablet again. "There's a particular symbol that kept showing up. It looks like a combination of Ra's sun disk and something to do with the river. We'll know we're close if we see anything that matches this along the banks."

Nathan, leaning lazily against the railing, suddenly straightened up. "Wait—are you saying we should just... keep an eye out for ancient Egyptian symbols carved into the side of the cliffs?"

"Exactly, I think that might work," Karly replied. Eli opened his mouth to protest but then paused. It sounded ridiculous, but nothing seemed impossible after what they'd seen last night.

As the boat continued down the Nile, they passed small islands dotted with ancient ruins, some half-sunken, into the river. Karly scribbled notes in her notebook, her eyes darting between her phone and the riverbanks.

Meanwhile, Nathan pulled out his phone and tried to zoom in on the distant cliffs and rocks that lined the river's edge, looking for any sign of the hieroglyphs they had seen on the tablet.

The rest of the group seemed oblivious to the groups quiet excitement. Their classmates lounged on the deck chairs, soaking up the sun or playing games on their phones, completely unaware that Eli, Karly, and Nathan were on the verge of discovering something extraordinary.

The hours passed slowly as the boat drifted deeper into the heart of Egypt. The sun climbed higher in the sky, creating shimmering reflections across the water.

The distant sound of birds echoed in the air, and now and then, they'd pass a small fishing boat, its lone captain waving at the tourists aboard the riverboat.

The air seemed to change as the boat rounded a wide bend in the river. It was subtle at first, a gentle cooling of the breeze, a slight dip in the temperature.

Then, without warning, a thick fog began to rise from the water's surface. Eli blinked repeatedly, "Is it supposed to get foggy like this in the middle of the day?" Karly shook her head, staring at the mist surrounding the boat.

"No. Not at all." "Come gather round kids" Mr Duncan said calmly, though fear could be seen on his face.

The once-clear view of the riverbank faded, replaced by a wall of swirling white fog. The boat's engines seemed too quiet. The classmates on deck fell silent, confused murmurs passing between them as they watched the sudden change in weather. Nathan stood up, squinting at the fog.

"This is weird, right?" Nathan asked. "Definitely weird," Eli replied.

The fog wrapped itself around the boat like a living thing, obscuring everything beyond a few meters. The palm trees, riverbank, and even the sun above were all gone, swallowed by the mist. The only sound now was the slow, steady sloshing of the Nile's waters against the side of the boat. Karly's grip tightened on her phone.

"I don't like this." Nathan chuckled nervously. "Hey, it's just fog. What's the worst that could happen?"

And then, through the swirling mist, something caught Eli's eye. "Wait, what is that?" he asked, pointing toward the left side of the boat. Nathan followed his finger, leaning over the railing. His eyes widened. "No way."

Karly hurried over, peering into the fog. At first, they saw nothing, just the gray swirls of mist. But then, as the boat drifted closer to the rocky cliffs on the riverbank, a faint glow appeared, flickering through the haze.

"Look!" Karly gasped. "On the cliffside! Do you see that?" Through the fog, they could make out the faint outlines of hieroglyphs carved into the rock. But these weren't ordinary symbols.

The carvings seemed to shimmer with a strange, golden light, flickering like flames in the mist. "It's the same symbol," Eli said. "The same one from the tablet." "We're getting closer. This must be where the map was pointing to," Karly said.

But a sudden jolt rocked the boat before they could process what they saw. The deck beneath their feet shuddered violently, sending a few of their classmates stumbling.

"What the, what's going on?" Nathan gasped, grabbing onto the railing to steady himself. The boat's engines sputtered, and a low grinding sound echoed below the deck. The captain's voice crackled over the loudspeaker, his tone tense. "Everyone, please remain calm. We seem to have hit something beneath the water."

Eli's eyes darted toward the river below. For a moment, he saw only the dark, murky water swirling in the boat's wake. But then, just below the surface, something glowed faint but unmistakable. An ancient Egyptian symbol, just like the ones on the cliff, glimmered beneath the water, pulsing with a strange, otherworldly light.

It was as if the river itself was alive with the power of the ancient gods, guarding something hidden deep below the surface.

"This can't be real," Nathan said, his voice shaky. "There's no way" But the evidence was right before them. The hieroglyphs on the cliff and the glowing symbol beneath the boat were all somehow connected.

They were on the verge of something huge: the map, the tablet, the treasure of Tutankhamun. And as the boat drifted closer to the bank, the fog swirling tighter around them, one thing became crystal clear: they were about to uncover a secret buried for thousands of years.

The sun had dipped below the horizon when the boat returned to the dock. The once-ominous fog had faded, leaving only the memory of the glowing hieroglyphs beneath the water and the sense of something ancient stirring.

The school group shuffled off the boat, tired but content with their day on the river, oblivious to the hidden secrets that only Eli, Karly, and Nathan had witnessed.

As they boarded the bus that would take them back to the hotel, Eli slumped into his seat, exhausted but too wired to relax.

His mind raced with the events of the day—the fog, the carvings glowing on the cliffside, the strange symbol flickering beneath the surface of the Nile. He glanced over at Karly, furiously typing notes into her phone, her face illuminated by the screen's blue glow.

Nathan plopped down beside Eli, throwing his backpack onto the seat beside him. "I can't believe what we saw today," he whispered excitedly, his voice barely contained and full of excitement.

"That glowing symbol in the water was exactly like the one from the tablet." "It's just crazy. That can't be a coincidence, right? The symbol, the map, the fog—it's all connected," Eli replied.

Karly leaned forward from her seat behind them. "It's more than just connected," she said, her voice serious. "Those hieroglyphs on the cliff weren't random. They were placed there for a reason, like a marker or a warning. And whatever's buried beneath the river is guarded by something powerful. I can feel it."

Nathan smirked. "Guarded by what? Ghosts?

Curses? Come on, Karly, it's just old carvings. Sure, the glowing stuff is freaky, but there's no such thing as magic or curses."

"Maybe not in the way we think of them, but ancient Egyptians believed the gods protected their treasures. They built traps, trials, and curses to keep people from sacred places. And the fact that we saw that symbol glowing beneath the water, something's still protecting whatever's down there," Karly replied.

The trio was buzzing with quiet energy when they reached the hotel. Too overwhelmed by what they'd experienced even to consider joining their classmates in the lobby for late-night snacks, they hurried up to their room, slipping inside and locking the door behind them.

Nathan collapsed onto one of the twin beds, his arms spread wide. "Okay, how long until we figure out what's down there and claim the treasure? I mean, we're practically real-life treasure hunters now."

Karly rolled her eyes but smiled. "You think it's going to be that easy? This isn't some video game. We're dealing with something ancient. We have to be careful." "Yeah, Nathan", Eli replied smartly, poking his tongue out at Nathan. Karly hit him with a pillow.

As they turned off the lights and settled into their beds, the soft buzz of Cairo at night drifted through the open window. The city, so alive with modernity, had secrets hidden in dark places.

# CHAPTER 4

## INTO THE DESERT

The sun had barely risen when Eli, Karly, and Nathan stood at the edge of the desert, just beyond the outskirts of Cairo. The golden sands stretched endlessly before them, rippling under the early morning sun like waves frozen in time. In the distance, the towering pyramids stood as silent towers, casting long shadows across the barren landscape.

"I can't believe we're actually doing this," Eli muttered, wiping the sweat from his forehead. The heat was already intense, and they hadn't even been out here for an hour. The group ensured they had enough water before leaving. "Yeah, well, this is what adventure looks like," Nathan replied with a grin, squinting into the distance. "Besides, this is what the map is pointing to, right? We're close."

Karly, the careful planner of the group, pulled out her notebook and the images of the tablet she had saved on her phone. "The hieroglyphs from yesterday were clear.

The clues lead to something buried near the pyramids. The map mentioned Anubis, and if we're right, we should be able to find the entrance to a hidden tomb or burial site around here."

The trio had slipped away from their classmates and teachers under the guise of exploring the desert near the pyramids as part of the school trip. No one had noticed their absence yet, but they knew they didn't have much time before someone realised they were missing.

The desert was unforgiving. The scorching heat beat down on them, the sand shifting beneath their feet with every step. It felt like the entire landscape was working against them, each dune was taller than the last, and the dry air burned in their throats as they pushed forward. Eli's nerves were already on edge.

"This is nuts," Eli groaned, kicking at the sand as they climbed another dune. "What if we get lost out here? We might die of thirst." "We won't," Karly said, her voice steady as she checked her phone. "Look, the pyramids are right there. If we keep them in sight, we won't lose our way. Besides, we're following the map. It's got to lead us to something."

Nathan grinned, wiping the sweat from his face with his sleeve. "Yeah, Eli. Relax. In the worst-case scenario, we find some ancient treasure and become legends. Not a bad way to go out, huh?"

Eli gave him a sideways glance. "I'd prefer not to go out at all, thanks." The heat was becoming unbearable, and the vast emptiness of the desert played tricks on your mind.

Finally, after what felt like hours, they stopped at the base of a towering dune. Karly checked her phone again, comparing the map's markings with their surroundings.

She looked up, scanning the horizon, her eyes locking onto a spot in the distance. "There," she said, pointing toward a different patch of sand. The dune's slope was uneven, and there was a strange formation of rocks half-buried in the sand.

"That's it? A pile of rocks?" Nathan asked. "It's more than that," Karly said, already marching forward. "Let's go check it out, you scaredy cats."

Eli followed, his eyes darting around the desert. The silence was unnerving, broken only by the occasional gust of wind that sent small swirls of sand dancing across the ground. When they reached the formation, Karly knelt down and brushed the sand away with her hand. Beneath the surface, more rocks emerged, smooth, dark, and etched with faint hieroglyphs.

"Well, this looks like it could be it," Eli said. Karly smiled excitedly. "Yes. Look at the markings. These are the symbols we saw on the tablet—the ones for Anubis." Nathan crouched down beside her, examining the stones. "So what now? How do we open it?" Karly glanced back at the pyramids, her mind racing.

"There's got to be some mechanism. The hieroglyphs said that only those 'pure of heart' could enter, which means there's a test." "When did we read that?" Nathan asked. "A test? You didn't mention anything about a test."

"We'll figure it out," Karly said confidently. She ran her fingers along the stones, tracing the symbols carefully. "These two are the symbols for Ra and Horus. They represent the sun and the sky, light and protection. There's got to be a way to combine them." Nathan stepped back, scanning the area. "Maybe there's something around here that we missed. A switch or a lever?"

But Eli wasn't so sure. He had a funny feeling that

this wouldn't be as easy as flipping a switch. The ancient Egyptians didn't just leave treasure lying around for anyone to find. There had to be something more. Karly stood up, brushing sand off her knees.

"I think the answer lies in the symbols themselves. The Eye of Horus symbolizes protection and healing, and Ra represents the sun. Maybe we need to solve a puzzle related to light or the sun."

Nathan scratched his head. "So, what? We wait for the sun to hit this spot?" Eli looked up at the sky. The sun was already high, beating down relentlessly. "I don't think we have time to wait around. There's got to be something else."

Karly closed her eyes in thought. She held up her phone, using the camera to zoom in on the hieroglyphs. "Wait, look at this. The symbols are positioned in a way that suggests movement. Like a path." "What do you mean? I don't get it." Eli asked, looking at her confused.

Karly pointed at the symbols. "The Eye of Horus is on the left, facing east, where the sun rises. Ra is on the right, facing west, where the sun sets. It's like they're pointing in opposite directions." Nathan fanned himself with a pamphlet, "Okay, but how does that help us?" "It's a clue! The sun rises and sets—light to dark, day to night. Maybe we need to recreate that transition somehow," Karly said.

Eli stared at the symbols, trying to make sense of them: the sun, light, transitions. And then it clicked. "What if it's about shadows?" he said suddenly.

"The ancient Egyptians used shadows in their architecture all the time. Maybe we need to cast a shadow on the right spot." "That makes sense! The Eye of Horus was meant to protect, but Ra was the god of the sun. If we combine the two..."

"Alright, but how do we cast a shadow in the desert?" Nathan asked. Eli looked down at the stone formation. "We use the stones. They're tall enough." They worked quickly, positioning themselves so the stones cast a long, narrow shadow over the hieroglyphs.

The sun beat down on their backs, and Eli could feel sweat trickling down his neck. But after a few tense moments, the shadow finally aligned perfectly with the symbol of Ra.

For a moment, nothing happened. Then, with a low rumble, the ground beneath them began to shake, causing the sand around them to almost dance. The stone formation shifted, revealing a small, hidden door at the base of the rocks.

The door was carved with more symbols of

Anubis, his jackal head staring up at them, his eyes cold and lifeless. Karly stepped back, her breath catching in her throat. "This looks like the entrance." They had found it, the entrance to the tomb.

But before they could celebrate, the ground trembled violently beneath their feet. The sand shifted, and the rocks began to crack.

"Look out!" Nathan shouted, backing away as the stones started to crumble. "Come on! We have to get inside!" Karly yelled out. But just as they pushed open the door, the ground split open beneath them, sending a cascade of sand and rocks tumbling into the abyss below.

# CHAPTER 5

## THE FIRST TRAP

The three coughed as they got to their feet and dusted themselves off. "Everyone okay??" Karly asked. Eli and Nathan nodded. The air inside the pyramid was dense, ancient, and damp. A corridor lay before the group, so in they went.

Once inside, it felt as though the world above had disappeared. There were no more winds or shifting sands—just an eerie silence that seemed to seep into their bones.

The passage was narrow, with walls pressing close around them, and the light from their phones barely cut through the inky blackness ahead.

Nathan tapped his phone flashlight to try and brighten the path in front of them, but it barely made a dent in the darkness.

"I didn't think it would be this dark," he said. Eli swallowed hard and glanced at the walls adorned with intricate carvings of Anubis, Horus, and Ra—their jackal, falcon, and human forms watching silently from the stone. "Feels like they're watching us," he whispered.

"They are," Karly replied. She ran her fingers along the carvings, tracing the ancient hieroglyphs. "These are protection spells. The gods were said to guard the tombs of the Pharaohs. If we've learned anything, these weren't just myths."

Eli shivered despite the warmth of the air around them. It was one thing to read about ancient Egyptian gods and curses in a textbook, but it was another to be inside the tomb where those gods had once been worshipped and feared.

Every step felt heavier, as though they were walking deeper into a place they didn't belong—a place that was meant to be forgotten.

"Let's keep moving," Nathan said, pushing ahead into the unknown. The corridor was long, stretching into darkness with no end in sight.

The flickering lights from their phones illuminated hieroglyphs on the walls, but there was little else. As they ventured deeper, the passage began to widen, and the stone walls arched upward, revealing a larger chamber ahead.

The three entered cautiously, their footsteps echoing on the stone floor. It was a vast room, the ceiling soaring high above them, decorated with more hieroglyphs that gleamed faintly in the light.

"Look at this," Karly whispered. She stepped forward, holding her phone up to one of the walls. "These carvings, they tell a story." Eli and Nathan joined her, peering at the intricate symbols etched into the stone.

The carvings depicted a journey, an ancient Pharaoh's quest for eternal life, guided by the gods. Anubis, the god of the underworld, appeared frequently in the images, his jackal head watching over the Pharaoh as he traversed the trials of the afterlife.

"It's a map," Karly said, her voice tinged with excitement. "A map of the trials the Pharaoh had to face. The Eye of Horus, Ra's sun, and Anubis scales were tests." Eli's pulse quickened. "So, we're walking through the same tests?"

"Exactly," Karly replied. "And we need to be ready for them." Standing at the far side of the room, Nathan kicked a small stone across the floor, watching it slide into the shadows. "Yeah, well, let's just hope we pass the tests, right?"

Suddenly, a loud click echoed through the chamber. Nathan froze, looking down at his foot, which had sunk into the floor. "Oh no." The room trembled.

The walls of the chamber began to shift slowly but unmistakably. The stones, once solid and still, started to move, sliding together, inching closer toward them. "Karly!" Eli shouted, panic rising in his chest. "What's happening?"

Karly's eyes darted around the room, scanning the carvings. "It's a trap! The walls, they're closing in on us!" Nathan backed up toward the center of the room, his face pale.

"I think I triggered something. I didn't mean to!" The grinding sound grew louder as the walls crept closer, narrowing the space around them. Dust and sand began to fall from the ceiling, and the floor beneath them rumbled.

"We need to figure this out!" Karly yelled. She ran to the nearest wall, frantically examining the hieroglyphs. "There has to be something here, something we can do to stop it!" The walls were moving faster now, the space shrinking around them. Eli's breath came in short gasps as he tried to stay calm, but the panic was overwhelming. There was no way out.

"Karly!" Nathan shouted, his voice desperate. "Do something!" Karly spotted a carving, the Eye of Horus, etched into the wall, glowing faintly. "That's it!" she cried, running toward the symbol.

"The Eye of Horus! It's a symbol of protection, and it's the key!" She pressed her hand against the Eye, tracing its outline with her fingers. The glowing symbol pulsed beneath her touch, and for a moment, everything stopped. The walls shuddered, and then silence.

The grinding noise ceased, and the walls came to a halt, inches from where they stood. Eli let out a breath he hadn't realised he'd been holding, his knees weak with relief. Nathan collapsed to the floor, his face pale and his breathing ragged.

Karly stepped back from the wall, her hand trembling. "The Eye of Horus, it saved us." For a moment, they stood in stunned silence. The tomb had tried to kill them, and they had barely escaped with their lives.

But the danger wasn't over yet. As the dust settled, Eli's gaze fell on the far side of the chamber, where a massive stone sarcophagus lay in the center of the room. It was carved from dark stone, its surface covered in intricate hieroglyphs, and the lid tightly sealed.

The symbols of Anubis were etched into the stone, his jackal head staring out from the surface with cold, lifeless eyes. A strange energy emanated from it, filling the room with an uneasy tension.

Karly stepped forward cautiously, her eyes locked on the sarcophagus. "This isn't just a tomb," she whispered. Nathan stood up, brushed the dust off his clothes, and stared at the sarcophagus. "Is that where the treasure is?"

"No, and it feels like it shouldn't be disturbed," Karly said. But Nathan couldn't resist. He took a step toward the sarcophagus, his eyes gleaming with excitement. "Come on, guys. This is it. This is what we've been looking for."

Karly grabbed his arm, her voice sharp. "No. We've come too far to make a mistake now. Whatever's in there, it's been sealed for a reason." Eli's voice trembled as he spoke. "Nathan, don't." But it was too late.

Nathan reached out and touched the sarcophagus, his fingers brushing the cold stone. The moment he made contact, the room seemed to shudder, a low rumble vibrating through the air.

The ground beneath their feet trembled once more, and a deep grinding sound echoed through the chamber, a sound that seemed to come from the walls themselves.

Eli stared at the sarcophagus. The hieroglyphs covering its surface began to glow faintly, pulsing with a strange, unnatural light. "Nathan," Karly said, "What did you do? Didn't your mum ever tell you not to touch things!?"

Before anyone could react, the lid of the sarcophagus shifted. The ancient stone groaned as the lid began to slide open, revealing a glimpse of the darkness within. And then, with a deafening crash, the lid fell to the floor. The three stepped back in terror; whatever lay inside was waking up.

# CHAPTER 6

## AWAKENING THE GUARDIAN

The heavy crash of the sarcophagus lid hitting the floor echoed through the chamber, sending tremors through the ground beneath their feet. The air in the tomb seemed to grow colder and icy-like, as if it had been holding its breath for thousands of years and had finally exhaled.

Eli took an instinctive step backward, his eyes locked on the open sarcophagus. The eerie glow of the hieroglyphs that had covered its surface had dimmed, leaving only the darkness within. A deep, suffocating silence filled the room as though the tomb was waiting for something to happen.

Nathan stood frozen, his hand still hovering over the edge of the stone coffin, his face drained of colour. "I didn't—I didn't mean to—" he stammered.

He looked to Karly for help, though she stood frozen also. "Nathan... step away from it. Slowly," Karly said with a trembling voice.

But before Nathan could move, a low, groaning sound began to rise from the depths of the sarcophagus. It wasn't the sound of stone or metal; it was something more profound and primal, like the earth groaning beneath their feet.

"That sound, it's coming from inside," Karly said in terror. Eli could hear the shift in the air, the thought of something terrible stirring just beyond the edge of their understanding.

He could hear the faint shuffling sound, like something moving inside the stone coffin. Nathan backed away, his face pale. "We need to get out of here," he whispered, his voice trembling. "Right now." But it was too late.

With a sudden, bone-chilling creak, a skeletal hand wrapped in decaying, ancient linen emerged from the sarcophagus, gripping the edge of the stone. The fingers were long, twisted, and inhumanly thin, covered in layers of dust and dirt. The amulets tied to its wrist gleamed faintly in the dim light, glowing with an ancient power that sent a jolt of terror through Eli's body.

He felt rooted to the spot, his legs refusing to

move as his brain screamed at him to run. Every instinct he had told him to flee, to escape this tomb, but his body was frozen in place by the overwhelming fear that something far more powerful than they had imagined was now awake. Karly took a shaky step backward and screamed, "That's, that's impossible."

The figure in the sarcophagus began to rise slowly and deliberately. Its entire form was shrouded in the wrappings of a mummy, but this was no ordinary mummy. This was a Guardian, a tomb protector bound by ancient magic to defend the treasures within.

Its movements were slow at first, almost mechanical, as though it hadn't moved in centuries. But as it stood to its full height, towering over them, it moved with a supernatural fluidity that made Eli's skin crawl.

"We need to go; who knows the way out, guys?" Nathan asked, his voice shaking as he took another step back. As the mummy's body fully emerged from the sarcophagus, a wave of energy pulsed through the chamber.

The air around them seemed to crackle with electricity, and the hieroglyphs on the walls began to glow once more, brighter this time, as though the

Guardian's presence was charging them.

Eli felt the power surging through the tomb, the same ancient force that had been dormant for thousands of years flowing through the Guardian. It wasn't just a relic; it was alive.

"Run!" Karly shouted, finally breaking the spell of fear that had gripped them all. The group bolted, sprinting toward the door at the far side of the chamber. Eli's legs felt like lead as he ran, his heart pounding in his ears.

The walls seemed to close in around them, the hieroglyphs glowing brighter as the Guardian stepped out of the sarcophagus, its hollow eyes locked on them.

Karly skidded to a stop as they reached the doorway, her eyes darting frantically across the walls. "We can't just leave! There's a way to stop it— we must figure it out!" Nathan glanced back at the Guardian, advancing toward them with slow, deliberate steps. Its decaying body moved with unnatural speed, its movements eerily smooth despite its ancient appearance.

"How do we stop something like that?" Eli yelled. "There has to be a clue. Anubis—the Guardian is tied to him. We need to find something related to Osiris that can neutralise it." "The amulet," Eli said suddenly, his mind flashing back to the stories they had read about the tombs. "The amulet of Osiris—if we find it, it can stop the Guardian." "Yes! The amulet is the key, it can calm the spirit. We have to find it, or it won't stop coming," Karly said.

Nathan groaned, glancing nervously at the approaching mummy. "And where exactly are we supposed to find that?" Eli's gaze shot to the far wall, where another series of hieroglyphs caught his eye. They were different from the others, more significant, more prominent.

Carvings of Osiris, the god of the afterlife, stood proudly in the centre, surrounded by symbols of protection and guidance.

Karly followed his gaze. "It's there. The amulet is connected to that wall." Without another word, they raced toward the hieroglyphs. The sound of the Guardian's footsteps echoed behind them, growing faster and more determined with each passing second.

As they reached the wall, Karly ran her fingers over the carvings, searching for a hidden compartment, a switch, or anything that could reveal the amulet. Eli kept one eye on the advancing Guardian, its lifeless eyes glowing faintly as it drew closer.

"Come on, come on" Karly muttered, her hands shaking as she searched the carvings. "It's here; it has to be here." Nathan looked back at the Guardian, now only a few feet away. "Karly, we're out of time!"

The mummy's amulets glowed brighter, their ancient magic surging through the tomb, filling the air with impending doom. Then, with a soft click, the wall shifted.

Karly gasped as a small compartment opened in the stone, revealing a golden amulet resting inside. It was intricately carved, the symbol of Osiris etched into its surface, and it pulsed with a faint, otherworldly glow.

"This is it," Karly breathed, carefully lifting the amulet from its resting place. "This is what we need." But before they could react, the ground beneath them began to tremble again.

The walls groaned as cracks appeared in the stone, and the entire chamber shook violently. "The tomb's collapsing!" Nathan shouted, his voice filled with panic. "Use the amulet! Stop the Guardian before it's too late!"

Karly was clutching the amulet tightly in her hands. She turned to face the advancing mummy, her eyes locked on its hollow gaze.

The Guardian was only a few feet away now, its skeletal hands reaching out toward them, the glow of its amulets intensifying with every step.

With a deep breath, Karly raised the amulet of Osiris high above her head, her voice steady as she called out in ancient Egyptian, the words flowing from her lips as though she had spoken them her entire life.

The amulet glowed brighter, casting a warm, golden light that filled the chamber. The Guardian froze in its tracks, its body trembling as the amulet's magic washed over it.

The power of Osiris surged through the air, calming the ancient spirit and forcing it back into submission. The glow of the mummy's amulets dimmed, and the light faded from its eyes. With a soft, defeated sigh, the Guardian collapsed to the ground, its body crumbling into dust.

Eli let out a breath of relief, his entire body shaking with exhaustion. Nathan slumped against the wall, his face pale and his chest heaving. Karly suddenly yelled, "Woohoo, how'd you like that, mummy!" Rocks began to fall from the roof.

With the amulet of Osiris clutched tightly in Karly's hand, the trio raced toward the exit, dodging falling debris as the tomb continued to crumble. The sound of the collapsing stone filled the air, and the ground shook beneath their feet, but they pushed forward, desperate to escape the wrath of the tomb.

As they reached the entrance, Eli glanced back one last time at the now-silent sarcophagus. The Guardian had been defeated, but the tomb was far from finished with them.

Just as they exited, the entrance collapsed behind them, sealing the tomb and its secrets forever.

# CHAPTER 7

## THE PHARAOH'S PUZZLE

The air outside the tomb was thick with dust as Eli, Karly, and Nathan stumbled away from the collapsing entrance. The ground beneath them continued to tremble, and the distant rumbling of the tomb's destruction echoed through the desert. Sand whirled around them, carried by the relentless wind, but none of them seemed to notice. They were too consumed by the shock of what had just happened.

Nathan bent over, hands on his knees, panting heavily. "I thought we were done for back there," he gasped, wiping the sweat from his brow. "I'm so thirsty," Karly replied. Eli collapsed onto the sand, his legs shaking from the adrenaline and fear. "We almost were," he muttered, his chest still heaving.

"That Guardian, mummy, whatever you want to call it, can you believe we just fought that! Did anyone get a photo of it?" Eli asked.

Karly sat beside him, clutching Osiris's amulet tightly in her hand. "At least we stopped it," she said, "The amulet worked." "Thanks for your quick thinking, Karly," Nathan said.

Eli stared at the golden amulet that now seemed much more powerful. "Yeah, but what now? The tomb's collapsing, and we still don't know where the treasure is."

Nathan finally straightened up, looking over at the entrance of the tomb. Dust and debris were still settling around the collapsed stones, and it was clear that they couldn't go back inside, even if they wanted to.

"We need to figure out where this map is leading us. The Guardian was just the start. There's more down here." Karly took a deep breath, finally loosening her grip on the amulet.

"There's always more," she whispered. "But we're running out of time." Eli glanced over at Karly. "What do you mean?"

She shook her head, her eyes filled with worry. "This tomb... everything we've seen so far. It's part of a bigger trial. The Pharaoh's treasure, the curse, it's all connected to Tutankhamun, and if we don't figure out how to solve this next puzzle, we will never find it."

Nathan looked around the desert, a faint grin tugging at the corners of his lips. "Yeah, as long as we don't wake up any more mummies, I think we'll be fine."

"Let's just get back to the group for today," Eli told Karly and Nathan. We can figure this out later." Nathan gave a half-hearted shrug. "Yeah, you're right. We can carry on tomorrow. Plus, I'm dying for a drink of cold water." They moved quickly but quietly across the sand, making their way back toward the school group, who were probably still blissfully unaware of the day's events.

The trio made their way through the lively streets of Cairo, the afternoon sun beating down as the city buzzed with activity. Cars honked, vendors shouted their wares, and the smell of freshly baked bread and spices filled the air.

Eli, Karly, and Nathan moved quickly, dodging pedestrians and the occasional stray cat as they headed toward the square where they knew their classmates would be.

When they finally reached the busy plaza, they spotted their school group huddled around a local guide explaining the history of a nearby marketplace. Some students stood near the fountain, cooling off in the shade of the trees, while others snapped photos of the vibrant market stalls filled with colourful fabrics, spices, and souvenirs.

"Hey, where've you been?" one of the students asked, sipping from a bottle of water as they approached.

"Just checking out the sights," Karly said with a small smile, her tone casual despite the wild reality of what they had just escaped. No one pressed them for details, too preoccupied with the excitement of being in the middle of Cairo's afternoon bustle.

They lingered with the group for a while, listening to the guide as she talked about the history of the nearby mosques and the ancient streets of Cairo. The sun was high in the sky, and the heat was starting to wear on them.

Eli wiped the sweat from his mouth, barely paying attention. His mind was elsewhere, still turning over the mysteries of the tomb.

Finally, the teacher announced it was time to head back to the hotel. The walk through the city was quieter now. Although the afternoon was still hot, the noise of the bustling streets began to fade as they reached the quieter area where their hotel was located. The cool air inside felt like a relief when they arrived at their rooms.

Without speaking, they each collapsed onto their beds, the day catching up with them. Eli lay there, staring at the ceiling, distant traffic humming in the background.

Despite the city still bustling outside, his mind remained in the tomb, thinking of the dangers they had faced, and the ones they might still have to face. As exhaustion took over, they drifted off into much-needed sleep.

Nathan and Eli woke the following day and went to find Karly, unable to locate her in her room. They headed downstairs, finding Karly in the food hall, frantically scrolling through her phone. "Hey, Karly," Nathan said.

Karly pointed to the symbols she had photographed from the tablet without looking up. "There's another chamber deeper into the pyramid. The hieroglyphs we saw earlier were just the beginning. We still need to solve the Pharaoh's Puzzle."

Eli's heart sank at the thought of venturing deeper into the pyramid. They had barely escaped the last trial with their lives, and now they were heading toward another one. But he knew there was no turning back. Not now. Not when they were so close. "Ok, so let's head back; the group didn't even notice us gone yesterday," Nathan said excitedly. The three grabbed their things and left the hotel, heading back across the sand dunes.

They found the half-buried pyramid again and moved toward the far end of the pyramid's ruins, where the next chamber was supposed to be hidden. Karly stopped suddenly as they approached the pyramid's base, looking around at the sandy ground. "This is it," she said.

Eli looked down and saw what she meant. The sand in front of them was different—darker, smoother. It looked as though it had been disturbed recently like something was buried beneath the surface.

Nathan knelt and brushed away some of the sand, revealing a series of stone slabs carved with intricate hieroglyphs. "Looks like another puzzle," he said. "This is it. The Pharaoh's Puzzle," Karly said. The slabs were arranged in a grid, each one marked with a different symbol—some familiar, like the Eye of Horus and the sun disk of Ra, and others more cryptic, their meanings lost to time. There were six slabs in total, each one connected to the others by faint lines carved into the stone, forming a web of interlocking symbols.

Karly chewed her lip, her eyes darting between the slabs. "The symbols are tied to the Pharaoh's journey through the afterlife. It's a test of knowledge and wisdom. We need to find the right combination to unlock the next chamber."

Nathan grinned, his usual confidence returning. "Alright, no problem. We've been cracking these codes all week. How hard can it be?"

But Karly wasn't smiling. She reached out and touched one of the slabs, her fingers tracing the outline of the Eye of Horus. "It's not just about solving it," she said softly. "It's about understanding it. The Eye of Horus represents protection, but it also represents sight—the ability to see beyond what's in front of you."

"So, we need to see something beyond the symbols?" Eli asked. "Yes. The symbols are just the surface. We must find the connections between them, like the story they're telling."

Nathan came and knelt beside the other two, "So what's the story?" Karly took a deep breath and pointed to the first symbol, the Eye of Horus. "The Eye is the beginning. It represents the Pharaoh's protection as he begins his journey through the afterlife. But he can't make it on protection alone.

He needs guidance." She pointed to the next symbol—Ra's sun disk. "Ra is the sun god, the guide through the sky. He represents light, knowledge, and the path forward."

"So, we need to follow the path of the Pharaoh's journey. The Eye of Horus for protection, Ra for guidance, what comes next?" Karly pointed to the third symbol, a pair of scales. "Anubis, the god of death and judgment. The Pharaoh must be judged before he can pass into the afterlife. Only those pure of heart can continue."

"So, if we mess this up, we're getting judged by Anubis?" Nathan asked. Karly didn't answer. She was already focused on the fourth symbol, a scarab beetle. "The scarab represents Khepri, the god of rebirth. It's the final step of the journey, a rebirth into the afterlife." Eli looked at the remaining two symbols, a pair of crossed sceptres and a feather. "What about these?"

"The crossed sceptres represent power, the Pharaoh's right to rule in life and death. The feather, that's the Feather of Ma'at, the goddess of truth and balance. It's the final judgment. If the Pharaoh's heart is lighter than the feather, he can pass into the afterlife." Nathan glanced nervously at the symbols. "And if it's not?"

For a long moment, they sat in silence, staring at the puzzle before them. The ancient trial seemed dangerous, and the group was unsure if they could do it. This test had been designed to keep people out, to protect the treasures buried deep within the pyramid.

"So, how do we do this?" Nathan asked, his voice low. Karly took a deep breath and placed her hand on the Eye of Horus. "We start with protection."

The slab beneath her hand shifted slightly, and the faint glow of the hieroglyphs grew brighter. Encouraged, she moved to the next symbol, the sun disk of Ra, and pressed it with equal care. The stone responded, its glow matching that of the Eye.

The slab beneath her hand shifted slightly, and the faint glow of the hieroglyphs grew brighter. Encouraged, she moved to the next symbol, the sun disk of Ra, and pressed it with equal care. The stone responded, its glow matching that of the Eye.

But she hesitated when she reached the final two symbols, the crossed sceptres and the feather. "Something's not right," she whispered. "The Pharaoh's heart, it must be weighed against the Feather of Ma'at. If the balance isn't right, the trial will fail." "But how do we know if it's balanced?" asked Eli. Karly shook her head, her eyes wide with fear. "I don't know."

Karly swallowed hard, her hand hovering over the crossed sceptres. "If I press the wrong symbol..." Nathan placed his hand on her shoulder, his voice soft. "We trust you, Karly. You've gotten us this far. Whatever happens, we're in this together." Karly's hand was still trembling as she pressed the crossed sceptres.

Then, with a deep, echoing rumble, the ground beneath their feet began to shake. The slabs shifted, and the lines connecting the symbols glowed brightly, filling the chamber with a blinding light.

Eli shielded his eyes as the puzzle began to unlock, the ancient magic surging through the stones. When the light faded, the ground beneath them gave way, sending them tumbling into the darkness below.

# CHAPTER 8

## SCARABS AND SHADOWS

Eli felt the air rush past him as he tumbled into the dark, the ground giving way beneath his feet. His stomach lurched as gravity pulled him into the depths of the pyramid.

He tried to reach out, but there was nothing to grab, only the cold, damp air whirling around him as he fell. Then, with a heavy thud, Eli landed hard on something solid.

Pain shot through his body as he hit the stone floor, his breath knocked from his lungs. For a moment, everything was a blur: the sound of the collapse above, the sensation of being weightless, and now the hard impact that left him dazed and gasping for air.

"Nathan! Eli! Are you okay?" Karly's voice called

out from somewhere nearby, breathless and full of concern. Eli groaned, pushing himself up onto his elbows, his body aching from the fall. "I think so," he managed to say, though his voice was shaky. His phone's flashlight had gone out during the fall, leaving him completely blind.

"Where's Nathan?" Karly asked, her voice filled with worry as she shuffled closer to Eli in the dark. "I'm here," Nathan said, surprisingly steady given the situation. "Just bruised. I think we all hit the floor hard. You guys alright?"

"Yeah, I think so," Eli replied, though the sharp pain in his ribs suggested otherwise. He winced as he tried to stand, the tight, heavy air of the underground chamber pressing in on him from all sides.

He fumbled for his phone and flicked on the flashlight, the beam cutting through the thick darkness to reveal the stone floor beneath them.

Karly's light flickered on next, and then Nathan's. The narrow beams of light swung around, illuminating their surroundings. They had landed in what appeared to be an underground tunnel, the walls lined with rough stone blocks that seemed to extend endlessly in both directions. The ceiling was low, barely high enough for them to stand, and it smelt of earth and decay.

"Where are we?" Nathan asked, sweeping his light across the tunnel. "This doesn't look like part of the pyramid." Eli shook his head, trying to clear his thoughts. The fall had disoriented him.

They were deep underground, far below where they had been moments ago. "It's part of the tomb," he said, his voice hoarse. "The Pharaoh's Puzzle, it must have been a trap."

Karly was inspecting the walls, her hands running over the rough stone. "This was designed to lead us here. The puzzle wasn't about finding the treasure— it was about taking us deeper into the tomb."

Nathan groaned. "Deeper? Are you serious? How deep does this thing go?" Karly's eyes narrowed as she scanned the tunnel. "Deep enough to keep people out."

Eli's flashlight flickered over the floor, illuminating something strange: small cracks and openings in the stone, almost like tiny fissures running along the walls and floor. He knelt to get a better look, shining his light into one of the gaps.

But before he could say anything, a soft rustling sound reached his ears, low and constant, like the sound of dry leaves being swept across the ground. Karly's head snapped toward the noise. "What is that?"

Nathan stepped closer, his light following the sound. "It's coming from the walls..." As if on cue, something small and dark crawled out of one of the cracks in the wall—a scarab beetle, its hard shell gleaming faintly in the light. It moved quickly, skittering across the floor before disappearing into another crack. Karly gasped. "It's a scarab."

Nathan remembered the stories they had heard about Khepri, the god associated with the scarab beetle, rebirth, renewal, and the rising sun. But the scarabs were also guardians of the tombs, protecting what lay within from anyone who dared to disturb the rest of the dead. Eli groaned, taking a step back from the wall. "Great, more creepy crawlies. Let's hope these aren't dangerous."

But before they could react, the rustling sound grew much louder. Eli's flashlight flickered across the walls again, and his heart nearly stopped when he saw them.

Dozens, no, hundreds of scarabs were now pouring out of the cracks, swarming across the stone floor in a thick, writhing mass. Their hard shells clacked together as they moved, creating a low, ominous hum that filled the air. "Run!" Karly shouted, her voice high with panic. She backed away from the advancing wave of beetles, her phone light trembling in her hand.

Without thinking, they turned and sprinted down the narrow tunnel, their phone lights bouncing wildly as they raced to escape the approaching swarm. The scarabs' clattering legs echoed off the walls, growing louder with every passing second.

Eli's lungs burned with the effort, and his legs felt like lead as he pushed himself forward, desperate to stay ahead of the swarm. He could feel the heat of the beetles' mass behind him, their relentless movement filling the air with a suffocating sense of dread.

Up ahead, Karly led the way, her flashlight bouncing off the walls as she looked for a way out. "There has to be an exit!" she yelled. Nathan almost tripped, his hand brushing the wall to steady himself. "Just keep going!" he shouted, his voice shaky with fear.

The scarabs were catching up, flooding the tunnel like a moving river of shiny black shells and sharp legs. He could hear the clicking of their jaws and the scratching of their legs against the stone walls.

Then, just as the tunnel seemed to narrow further, Karly's light caught something, a dark opening in the wall up ahead. "There!" she shouted, veering toward the opening. "A side tunnel!" Eli followed her lead, his body aching from the strain of running. He could feel the scarabs nipping at his heels, their clattering shells echoing in his ears. The tunnel was narrowing, and he knew they had little time left.

As they reached the opening, Karly darted inside, followed closely by Nathan and Eli. The moment they were inside, Karly slammed her shoulder against the door-like slab of stone that had hidden the entrance, sealing it shut behind them.

The tunnel was filled momentarily with the deafening sound of the scarabs scratching and clattering against the stone slab. But after a few seconds, the noise began to fade, and the scarabs moved on, leaving the group alone in the darkness again.

Eli collapsed against the wall, his chest heaving as he struggled to catch his breath. Sweat dripped down his face, and his entire body trembled with exhaustion and fear. "That was too close," Karly gasped, her eyes wide with terror.

"Tell me about it. I never want to see another beetle for as long as I live," Nathan said. Eli closed his eyes, trying to calm his racing mind. "What was that?"

Karly shook her head, her face still pale. "Scarabs. They're connected to Khepri, the god of rebirth. But they're also guardians of the tombs. They protect what's buried here." Eli shuddered. "Protect it from what? Us?"

"Yes. The deeper we go, the more dangerous it gets. We need to be careful." They had barely escaped the Guardian, and the scarabs had nearly caught them.

Nathan sighed, pushing himself to his feet. "Alright, so what now? Do we sit here until we get eaten by something else?" Karly shook her head, her eyes scanning the tunnel ahead.

"No. We keep going. There's something deeper in the tomb, something we haven't found yet." "Deeper? How much deeper can we go?" Eli replied. Karly turned to him; her expression serious. "We're close, Eli. I can feel it. The treasure of Tutankhamun, the key to this entire mystery, it's down here, somewhere. We must find it."

Karly turned her phone light toward the end of the side tunnel. "Come on," she said through a drained yet excited voice. "There's more ahead." Eli and Nathan exchanged glances, their nerves raw from the chase, but they followed her lead, stepping deeper into the shadows of the tomb. The air was colder now, and the tunnel was narrower than before. The only sound was the soft shuffle of their footsteps on the stone floor and the distant echo of the scarabs moving elsewhere in the tomb.

After what felt like an eternity of walking, the tunnel opened into a small chamber. The air inside was colder still, and the walls were lined with more hieroglyphs, only this time, the carvings were more intricate and detailed.

Eli's phone light flickered over the walls, illuminating a set of statues, tall figures of Egyptian gods, their eyes fixed on the center of the room. In the middle of the chamber stood a large stone altar, and on it lay a golden chest, its surface adorned with carvings of Anubis and Horus.

Karly stepped forward cautiously, her eyes wide with awe. "This is it," she whispered. The Treasure of Tutankhamun.

"Wait, didn't we learn from last time about touching things we shouldn't?" Nathan asked. We survived, didn't we?" Karly responded with a sharp tone. As she reached for the chest, a low, rumbling sound echoed through the chamber, and the statues' eyes began to glow..

# CHAPTER 9

## THE CURSE AWAKENS

Karly's fingers hovered just above the surface of the golden chest. The gleaming metal reflected the faint light of their phone lights, casting an eerie glow around the room.

The chest was small but intricately detailed, with carvings of Egyptian gods and symbols of power covering every inch of its surface. At its centre was an image of Tutankhamun, standing proudly with the gods of Egypt surrounding him.

Eli felt a sense of dread wash over him as he stared at the treasure. This was it, the famous treasure of Tutankhamun. They had found it deep within the tomb's hidden chambers. "Careful, Karly," Eli warned, "We don't know what touching that thing might do." Karly glanced over her shoulder at him, her eyes wide with excitement and nervous energy. "This is what we came for, Eli," she whispered. "This is the treasure the map was leading us to."

Nathan, standing a few steps behind them, shifted nervously. His phone light flickered over the statues lining the walls of the chamber. Each figure seemed to be staring down at the chest, their stone eyes gleaming unnaturally.

Anubis, Horus, and Ra were all present, watching silently, their expressions frozen in eternal judgment. "I don't like this," Nathan muttered. "The statues, the way they're watching us. It's like they're waiting for something."

Eli felt the same uneasy sensation. The glowing eyes of the statues, the eerie stillness of the chamber, it was as if the room itself was alive, waiting for them to make a move.

Deep down, he knew this treasure wasn't just sitting there for them to take. There would be a price. Karly reached out for the chest, "I'm just going to open it; what's the worst that could happen," she whispered, almost to herself. "Let the mummies come."

Karly grabbed the edge of the chest and reefed it open as a deep, rumbling sound echoed through the chamber. The chest was overflowing, packed to the brim with ancient coins, their surfaces worn but still gleaming with the soft glow of aged gold. E

Each coin bore the imprint of pharaohs long forgotten, their faces stamped with hieroglyphs and symbols of power. The treasure glinted with a richness that seemed almost alive, shimmering as if it had been waiting for centuries to be uncovered.

Around the coins, gemstones of every color sparkled, their polished surfaces catching the light and casting fractured beams around the room.

Deep red rubies, rich purple amethysts, and vibrant emeralds were scattered like stars among the treasure, their edges cut into perfect facets. Some were as large as their fists, nestled together as though they had been collected from the tombs of kings, waiting to be admired once more.

But that wasn't all. Draped over the mound of gold and gems were necklaces of intricate design, their chains woven from thin strands of gold and silver.

Each necklace held enormous, glittering diamonds, their clarity so perfect that the light seemed to pass through them like liquid fire. The diamonds sparkled like frozen sunlight, casting dazzling reflections that danced on the chamber walls. Sapphires and topazes adorned the necklaces as well, their deep blues and yellows catching the light like fragments of the sky.

The ground beneath their feet trembled, sending small pebbles skittering across the floor. "Karly, stop!" Nathan shouted, his voice filled with terror and disbelief. The statues along the walls began to move, their stone limbs creaking and grinding as they came to life.

The once-frozen figures of the gods now towered over them, their glowing eyes fixed on the trio. Anubis, his jackal head tilting toward the chest, stepped forward, his massive stone paws scraping against the floor. Ra and Horus followed suit, their eyes blazing with a fierce, unnatural light.

"Oh no," Nathan breathed, backing away from the advancing statues. "This is bad. This is really, really bad." The treasure—this wasn't just a prize waiting to be claimed. It was a trap, a test set by the gods to protect what had been buried for millennia. "We need to get out of here!" Eli shouted, grabbing Karly's arm and pulling her back. "Now!"

But the moment he touched her, the statues froze, their glowing eyes locked onto him. A deep, low growl echoed through the chamber, and Eli's body went cold. The weight of the gods' gaze was suffocating, and he could feel the ancient power of the tomb. Karly clutched the amulet of Osiris tightly in her hand. "The curse, it's real," she yelled. "The gods are protecting the treasure. We've triggered it."

Nathan was already backing toward the door, his eyes darting between the statues and the treasure. "What do we do? How do we stop this?" The statues and the tomb were alive, and they had disturbed something far older and more powerful than they had imagined. The glowing eyes of the gods bore down on them, judging them and waiting to see what they would do next.

"We have to offer something back," Karly said. Eli turned to her, confused. "What do you mean?" She held up Osiris's amulet, her hand shaking. "The Pharaoh's treasure was meant to be protected for eternity. We can't just take it. We have to offer something in return, something worthy of the gods."

"It's the only way. We triggered the curse by trying to take it, but if we give something back, maybe we can stop it," Karly replied. Eli's heart sank. They had come all this way, fought through traps, awakened the Guardian, and were told they had to give up the treasure. But as much as it pained him, he knew Karly was right. The tomb wasn't going to let them leave with Tutankhamun's treasure. Not without a sacrifice.

"What do we give them?" Eli asked, his voice hoarse. Karly thought quickly, holding up the amulet. "This. The amulet of Osiris. It's the only thing powerful enough to balance the curse." Eli stared at the golden amulet in her hand, its surface gleaming faintly in the light of their phone lights. It had saved them from the Guardian, and now it was their only hope of escaping the tomb alive.

Nathan's face twisted in frustration. "But if we give up the amulet, we're defenseless. What if something else happens?" "We don't have a choice," Karly said back to him. Karly stepped forward and placed the amulet on the chest.

The moment it touched the surface of the golden treasure, a blinding light filled the chamber. Eli shielded his eyes, the intensity of the light overwhelming his senses. The room seemed to hum with energy momentarily, and the air grew warm, almost comforting.

When the light finally faded, Eli lowered his arm and blinked in shock. The statues had returned to their original positions, their eyes no longer glowing. The rumbling of the tomb had stopped, and it seemed the curse had been neutralised. Karly let out a shaky breath, her shoulders slumping with relief.

"Thank you, Tutankhamun," she said smartly, looking at Nathan and Eli for acknowledgment.

Eli's legs felt weak, and he collapsed onto the stone floor, his chest heaving with exhaustion. The tension and fear came crashing down at once, leaving him drained.

Nathan, still standing by the door, shook his head in disbelief. "I can't believe we just gave up the treasure. After all that." "We're alive, Nathan. That's worth more than any treasure," Karly replied with a silly look on her face. Deep down, he knew Karly was right. They had survived the tomb trials, which was the real victory.

As they prepared to leave the chamber, something caught Eli's eye. He turned toward the altar and saw something he hadn't noticed before, a golden sceptre half-hidden behind the chest. Its surface was engraved with intricate symbols, and at its top was the unmistakable image of the Eye of Horus.

"Look, what do you think that is? Was that there before?" Eli asked, pointing toward the altar. Karly and Nathan turned toward the altar, their eyes widening in surprise. "The sceptre," Karly said, stepping closer. "It's part of the treasure." "You think we're supposed to take that?" Nathan asked curiously.

The curse had been lifted, but the tomb was unpredictable. Still, something about the sceptre called to Eli as if it held the key to everything they had been searching for. "We have to; I can feel it calling to me", Eli said quietly, stepping forward. "It's important. I can feel it like an emotion."

Eli reached out and carefully lifted the sceptre from the altar. The moment his fingers closed around it, energy shot through his body.

It wasn't like the curses or traps they had encountered before, this felt different, stronger, as though the sceptre held power beyond anything they had encountered. For a moment, the chamber was still. The statues remained frozen in place, the treasure untouched. But then, with a sudden crack, the ground beneath them trembled again.

The ground cracked beneath their feet, and the ceiling began to crumble, sending chunks of stone crashing to the floor. The entire tomb collapsed around them, the sceptre's power unleashing the final curse. "We need to move!" Nathan shouted; his voice barely audible over the roar of the collapsing chamber.

Eli clutched the sceptre tightly as they raced toward the door, dodging falling debris and stumbling over the uneven ground. The statues of the gods were crumbling around them, their stone forms collapsing as the tomb gave way to the ancient magic that had been holding it together for centuries.

As they sprinted down the tunnel, the sound of the tomb's collapse followed them, growing louder and more intense with every step. Karly led the way, her phone light flickering in the darkness as they navigated the twisting tunnels.

The path seemed endless, the walls closing in around them as the ceiling continued to fall. Eli could feel the ground shaking beneath him, the sceptre's power pulsing through his veins, urging him to keep moving.

When it seemed like the tomb would collapse entirely, they burst through the final doorway, stumbling out into the open air of the desert. The cool night breeze hit Eli's face like a wave of relief, and he collapsed onto the sand, gasping for breath. Behind them, the entrance to the tomb crumbled, sealing the treasure and its curse forever.

They lay in the sand for a long moment, too exhausted to move. The stars twinkled in the clear desert sky, taking in the chaos they had just escaped.

The air was cool and calm, a far cry from the suffocating atmosphere of the tomb. Nathan let out a shaky laugh, his voice filled with disbelief. "Best school trip ever! Mummies, treasure, ancient gods, what else could you ask for."

He held up his phone, "I even got a picture of the treasure chest," he said. Karly laughed at him, shaking her head whilst panting.

The artifact's power pulsed faintly beneath his fingers, a reminder of the ancient magic they had just encountered. Was this really the end, the group thought to themselves?

# CHAPTER 10

## ANUBIS' JUDGEMENT

The desert air was cool and calm, and the moon hung low in the sky, casting a faint silver glow over the dunes. Eli, Karly, and Nathan lay sprawled across the cool sand, their bodies aching from the sprint out of the collapsing tomb. The dust from the crumbling entrance had settled, leaving only silence. Nathan lay in the sand, calm for now, though an overwhelming feeling sunk in. Eli felt it, too.

Eli stared at the golden sceptre in his hand, its intricate carvings glowing faintly in the moonlight. It was beautiful, almost mesmerising, but it pulsed with a strange energy like the artifact had a mind of its own. The sceptre had been buried deep within the tomb, hidden beneath layers of traps and curses, and now that it was in his hands, Eli couldn't help but wonder if they had made a terrible mistake by taking it.

"We should have left it behind," Karly said quietly, sitting up and hugging her knees to her chest. She was staring at the sceptre, too. "The treasure, the curse, it's all tied to that thing. The gods aren't going to let us walk away with it."

Nathan, lying flat on his back with his hands behind his head, groaned softly. "We barely made it out of there alive, Karly. I'm not going back in there to put it back."

Eli frowned, his fingers tightening around the sceptre. "We can't go back. The tomb collapsed. The only way out is through." Karly's gaze shifted to Eli, her expression grim. "Through what?" Eli didn't answer. Nathan sighed, sitting up and brushing the sand off his clothes. "What's the plan then? We hang around the desert until we figure out what to do next?"

Before anyone could answer, the ground beneath them rumbled. Eli shot to his feet. The sand beneath his shoes shifted, trembling slightly as if something beneath the surface was moving.

The night air, which had been so calm only moments before, had become angry. "What's happening?" Karly said, scared out of her mind. The rumbling grew louder, and the sand beneath their feet began to ripple.

"Look!" Nathan shouted, pointing toward the horizon. Eli and Karly spun around, looking at what Nathan pointed at. In the distance, emerging from the sand like a figure rising from the depths of the earth, stood the unmistakable silhouette of Anubis.

The jackal-headed god of the underworld loomed over the desert, his stone form towering above the dunes. His eyes, glowing with an eerie green light, were locked on them, and the faint outlines of scales, the symbol of judgment—were etched into the air beside him.

The sight of Anubis was terrifying. They all knew, without a doubt, that the final trial was upon them.

Nathan took a shaky step backward. "You've got to be kidding me. That thing's real? Look at the size of it!"

"We've disturbed the tomb. We've awakened the curse. Now we have to face Anubis' judgment," Karly said. "We have to prove ourselves," Karly continued, trembling. "Anubis is the judge of the dead. He weighs the heart against the feather of Ma'at to determine whether a soul is pure enough to enter the afterlife. If we're found unworthy..."

Nathan's face paled. "If we're found unworthy,

what?" Karly didn't answer, but the look in her eyes was enough. Eli understood. If they failed this trial, they wouldn't just lose the treasure; they might lose their lives. The treasure, the curse, the sceptre, everything was connected. The trials they had faced in the tomb led to this moment, the final judgment. But how could they prove themselves worthy?

Before Eli could voice his thoughts, the rumbling beneath the sand intensified, and the massive form of Anubis began to move. His stone feet, buried halfway in the sand, shifted as he stepped forward, his glowing eyes locked onto the three.

"Look out!" Nathan shouted, grabbing Karly's hand and pulling her toward a nearby dune. Eli followed close behind, his eyes wide with fear as the massive figure of Anubis continued to approach.

No matter how fast they fled, it was impossible to outrun the gods' judgment. The desert around them seemed alive, the sand rippling like waves under Anubis' piercing gaze.

The air buzzed with ancient energy, and Eli could feel the power of the underworld tightening its grip, drawing ever closer. As they reached the top of the dune, they skidded to a halt.

Before them, a massive stone platform had risen from the sand, glowing faintly in the moonlight. At its centre stood a set of scales identical to the ones Anubis was said to use in his judgments. The platform was carved with intricate hieroglyphs.

"I think this is it, guys; this is the trial," Karly said. The scales loomed ahead, the symbol of Ma'at, the goddess of truth and balance, etched into the stone beside them. This was the moment of judgment.

"What do we do with it, do you think?" Nathan asked. Karly turned to Eli, her eyes filled with uncertainty. "The sceptre, it's the key. It's tied to the treasure, the curse, everything. It's what Anubis wants." Eli stared down at the golden sceptre in his hand, its weight suddenly overwhelming.

The artifact pulsed faintly beneath his fingers as if urging him forward, calling him to complete the final trial.

Without a word, Eli stepped forward, his breathing rapid. He approached the scales, holding the golden sceptre tightly in his hand and placing it on one side of the balance. For a moment, nothing happened. Then, with a low, echoing rumble, the scales began to tip, shifting slowly as they weighed the sceptre against the weight of their deeds, intentions, and worthiness.

Eli could feel the god's eyes watching, judging, as

the scales shifted. Every breath felt like a struggle.

"We've disturbed something very sacred," Karly whispered, her voice trembling. "This treasure, these artifacts were never meant to leave the tomb." Eli knew she was right. The treasure wasn't theirs to take. But how could they prove to Anubis that they were worthy of leaving with their lives?

The scales tipped further, and the sceptre began to sink lower. The weight of their actions was too great, too much greed and disturbance of the sacred. They had trespassed into the realm of the gods, and now they were paying the price.

"No!" Karly shouted, stepping forward. "There has to be another way!" Eli's mind raced as he looked around, searching for a solution. The sceptre, treasure, and curse were all connected, but how could they prove their worth?

Then, a thought struck him. The treasure wasn't the answer. The key to passing the trial wasn't the treasure they had found but the sacrifice they were willing to make.

"I know what to do," Eli said. Eli reached for the sceptre and lifted it from the scales. The balance tipped slightly, but the side weighed down by their deeds remained low. "We have to give it back," Eli said, his voice steady but filled with urgency. "We have to return the treasure to the tomb." Nathan's eyes widened in disbelief. "Are you serious? After everything we went through to find it?"

Eli nodded, "It's the only way. We can't leave with it. The gods won't let us." Karly stepped forward. "Eli's right. We've disturbed something sacred. We need to return the treasure to the tomb and prove that we respect the gods' judgment."

Nathan groaned, rubbing his temples. "This is insane, but fine. Let's do it. I may be the reason the gods are angry," Nathan said. "What do you mean?" Karly asked quickly. Nathan reached into his pocket and pulled out a stunning blue gem.

The gem shimmered with a deep oceanic blue, its surface smooth and radiant, encircled by intricately crusted gold edges that gleamed like sunlit waves against a tranquil sea. The three of them were almost mesmerized by it. "Nathan! Why?" Karly said to him. "I don't know! I wasn't thinking, and it looks so beautiful," he said. Karly snatched it out of his hands, shaking her head.

Together, the three stepped forward, carrying the sceptre and the small, precious gem Nathan had taken from the chamber. The platform hummed with energy as they approached, and Anubis's presence seemed to grow stronger, his glowing eyes watching their every move.

With careful hands, they placed the treasure on the scales, offering it back to the gods and returning it to the tomb where it belonged. Nothing happened immediately, but then, with a soft click, the scales tipped once more, and the weight of the treasure began to balance. The glow from the scales brightened, filling the air with a warm, golden light.

Anubis, the towering god of the underworld, stood still, his eyes no longer glowing with judgment. The presence of the gods, the curse of the tomb, seemed to recede. Anubis began disappearing before them in a gentle sandstorm and into thin air. Eli let out a breath of relief, his body trembling with exhaustion. They had passed the trial.

They had proven themselves worthy, not by taking the treasure, but by respecting what they had found. As the light from the scales faded, the stone platform began to sink back into the sand, the trial complete. "I'm so happy that it is all over," Karly said joyfully.

The tomb, treasure, and gods had all been more than he had ever imagined. And though they had survived the trial, he knew that the memory of this adventure would stay with them forever. Nathan let out a shaky laugh, running a hand through his hair. "Well, that was the scariest thing I've ever been through. But we made it. Reckon anyone will ever believe us?" Nathan asked. "No, I doubt it very much" Karly replied.

Nathan pulled his phone from his pocket and opened it, quickly flicking to the images. There it was, a beautiful picture of Tutankhamun's treasure chest with golden coins and forgotten gems and diamonds. "Nathan, what are you doing?" Eli said suddenly. Nathan closed his phone quickly and returned it to his pocket. "Nothing, let's go," he replied.

They had survived Anubis's final trial, and they had proven themselves worthy. But as they began to walk away from the platform, back toward the safety of the desert, Eli couldn't shake the feeling that the gods were still watching.

And somewhere, deep beneath the sand, the tomb of Tutankhamun remained, guarding its secrets for another thousand years.

# CHAPTER 11

## THE GODS' WRATH

The desert was silent as Eli, Karly, and Nathan trudged across the dunes, their footsteps heavy in the cool sand. The golden glow of the moon was now high in the sky, casting long shadows across the endless expanse.

Though they had survived Anubis' judgment and returned the treasure, the sense of relief they expected never came. Something was still terribly wrong.

Eli's skin tingled with unease, and each breath felt harder. The sceptre might have been returned and the treasure left behind, but it felt like the desert wasn't done with them yet. Karly walked beside him, her face pale in the moonlight. She had barely spoken since they had left the platform. Nathan, who usually found a way to joke about everything, was also quiet, his eyes darting nervously to the horizon every few seconds.

"We did what we were supposed to, right?" Nathan finally asked, his voice concerned. "We gave back the treasure. We passed the test. So why does it feel like we're still in trouble? You two feel that, right?"

"Who knows, it did seem pretty intense that last part, so probably, though you're right, I feel like it isn't over," Karly said through breathless pants.

Karly stopped walking and turned to face them suddenly, her eyes filled with worry. "Something's coming," she whispered. Eli and Nathan turned toward the horizon, following Karly's gaze. At first, there was nothing—just the vast emptiness of the desert stretching out before them.

But then, in the distance, a faint glow appeared. It was initially small, a flicker of light against the dark sky, but it grew fast.

It spread across the horizon like wildfire. It wasn't the warm, golden light of the treasure chamber or even the glow of the scales they had faced during Anubis' judgment. This was different—angrier, more intense. The light flickered and pulsed, swirling in the distance like a storm brewing on the horizon.

Karly's voice trembled. "It's the gods again, and I don't think they're happy!"

"What do you mean, the gods? We gave everything back. We passed the test!" Karly shook her head, her voice shaking. "We gave back the treasure, but we woke something ancient up. The gods—Ra, Isis, Osiris—they aren't happy. We disturbed their tomb, their resting place. We're still being judged."

The wind began to pick up, swirling the sand around them in spirals. The glow on the horizon grew brighter, and the storm-like energy surged forward, racing toward them with a speed that scared them all.

"We need to move!" Nathan shouted, grabbing Karly's hand and pulling her forward. Eli was already sprinting ahead of them, his footsteps kicking up clouds of sand as they fled.

The storm of light and energy behind them grew closer, and a deep rumbling sound came, like thunder rolling across the desert. "Keep going!" Karly shouted over the roar of the wind. "We can't stop!" But Eli knew that the gods would find them even if they ran for miles. There was no escaping their judgment. The only way to survive was to please them, to find some way to prove that they meant no harm.

The storm was upon them now, the light swirling around them like a whirlwind of divine energy. Eli could barely see through the blinding glow, but he could make out the faint shapes of figures in the storm.

Ra, his sun disk blazing bright, Isis with her wings outstretched, and Osiris, towering and powerful. The gods descended slowly in front of the three, their presence overwhelming and terrifying. The storm's wind roared in their ears, and the light grew brighter until it was almost blinding.

Suddenly, the sand beneath their feet shifted, and Eli, Karly, and Nathan were thrown to the ground by the force of the wind. Eli coughed, spitting out sand as he pushed himself up on his hands and knees. The storm was swirling around them, trapping them in a circle of light and sand, the gods' figures looming above.

"I'm not sure what we do now," Karly yelled desperately, staring at the gods. They must want something from us," Nathan said. Yeah, hopefully not our lives!" Eli replied. Eli stood, struggling against the howling wind while shielding his face from the sandstorm. We need to show them we understand. That we respect their power, their legacy."

"How do you suggest we do that!?" Karly screamed as Ra began to move toward her. They weren't after the treasure. They had already returned it. This was about something more profound. The gods wanted respect and reverence. They wanted to know that their power, their presence, was still honoured.

Eli stepped forward, raising his hands toward the glowing figures of Ra, Isis, and Osiris. The wind seemed to quiet briefly, and the swirling light slowed as if the gods were watching, listening.

"We came here in search of treasure," Eli shouted, his voice firm but filled with reverence. "But we understand now, this tomb, this desert, this legacy, it doesn't belong to us. It belongs to the gods, the Pharaohs, and the ancient ones who built it. We disturbed it, and we were wrong. But we honour it now. We return it to you."

For a moment, the storm paused. The wind stopped, and the light dimmed slightly as the towering figures of the gods hovered above them, their eyes glowing with ancient power. Eli's gaze locked on the figures above. "We respect your judgment. We ask for your forgiveness; we beg for it. We're just a few school kids playing around, and we now understand."

The silence that followed was deafening. Eli held his breath, waiting for a sign, anything that would tell them if they had succeeded.

Then, slowly, the storm began to fade. The glowing light that had surrounded them dimmed, and the swirling winds subsided. The towering figures of Ra, Isis, and Osiris began to retreat, their forms growing fainter as they dissolved back into the horizon. Nathan and Karly looked at each other with tensioned smiles before falling back into the sand dunes in a heap.

"The storm, the gods, the treasure, we did it all, I think that worked," Eli celebrated, jumping in the air. Karly and Nathan were too exhausted to speak another word. The cool breeze gently stirred the sand around them. The air was calm now, unlike when they had entered the tomb.

"No one would ever believe this," Eli said. "I can't believe that work; maybe they figured it was too easy if some school kids could get to the treasure,", Karly said.

"We didn't take the treasure. We gave back what wasn't ours. That's what saved us." The three nodded in agreement. "Well, that was the closest I've ever been to getting smited by a god. Let's not do that again," Nathan laughed. Karly glanced at the horizon, where the first light of dawn was beginning to break. "We should get back to the river. The others will wonder where we are if we don't rock up to the boat this morning."

"I could sleep for three days, I think; it felt like time sped up with all that we just went through," Nathan said. The danger was over, and they had passed the final test. Now, all that remained was to return to the real world, leaving the gods and their tomb behind.

As they made their way back across the desert, the memory of the gods' wrath still fresh in their minds, Eli couldn't help but glance over his shoulder at the distant ruins of the tomb. The gods had spared them this time, but their judgment would forever linger in the dese

# CHAPTER 12

## BACK TO REALITY

The first rays of dawn stretched across the horizon as Eli, Karly, and Nathan trudged through the cool desert sands. The gods' once-overwhelming presence had faded into the calm of the early morning, and the oppressive weight of their judgment had lifted.

The desert now seemed peaceful, almost serene, in the soft light of day. They had survived. They had faced ancient curses, mummies, and trials set by the gods themselves, and now they were walking away from the tomb, alive and hopefully free of the curse.

The Nile shimmered faintly in the distance, a ribbon of blue that promised safety, comfort, and a return to the life they had left behind. The school group was probably waking up soon, preparing for another day of sightseeing, completely unaware of the monumental journey the three had undertaken in the last few hours.

Karly walked beside Nathan, her face calm. Her eyes were fixed on the glistening river ahead, though Eli knew her mind was still turning over the night's events. She had always been the most thoughtful of the three of them, constantly trying to piece together the bigger picture. This adventure, though, had tested even her considerable knowledge of Egyptology.

Eli, however, seemed more than ready to leave everything behind. His usual demeanour had returned now that the immediate danger had passed, and he walked ahead of them, occasionally glancing back with a grin. "I mean, can you believe it? We just survived the wrath of the gods. How many people can say that?"

Nathan let out a tired chuckle. "Not many. But I think I'm okay with that." Karly smiled faintly but didn't say anything. She had a faraway look in her eyes like she was still trying to process what had happened. After what felt like hours, they finally reached the banks of the Nile. The river flowed steadily, its surface glistening in the sunlight. Their school's river cruise boat was docked not far from where they had left it.

"You three, over this way, please", the teacher yelled toward them. Nathan turned quickly with a silly look on his face, "The teacher doesn't even know we were missing; good one, Mr. Duncan," Nathan laughed at the other two.

"We could be mummies right now and our teacher would be on the boat, talking about things he probably doesn't have a clue about with three missing children." Eli laughed loudly. Karly stared at him, not sure whether to laugh or cry.

Eli let out a sigh of relief as they approached the boat. He hadn't realized just how much he longed for the mundane comfort of normal life until now. He wanted nothing more than to sleep for days, far away from mummies, scarabs, and ancient curses. Nathan, already climbing up the boat's gangplank, stretched his arms above his head. "Can't wait to hit the breakfast buffet. They better have pancakes."

Karly lingered behind for a moment, looking back toward the desert. Eli stopped beside her, following her gaze.

In the distance, the sand dunes stretched endlessly, hiding the tomb and its secrets beneath their golden surface. The ancient gods, the treasure of Tutankhamun, the trials they had faced, it all seemed so far away now, like a story from another world.

The experience had been overwhelming, but it had also been exhilarating. They had faced unimaginable danger, but they had also uncovered something extraordinary, something that most people would never even dream of. "It's not something we'll ever forget," Eli said. Karly smiled, her eyes still on the horizon. "No, it's not."

Karly trudged behind Eli as they returned to the boat and jumped aboard. As they climbed aboard, the familiar sounds of the other students laughing, talking, and getting ready for the day's excursions felt like a strange return to reality. Like nothing in the world could describe what had just happened to their classmates.

Nathan was already sitting at one of the tables, a plate of food in front of him, as if nothing out of the ordinary had happened. He waved them over with a grin. "Come on, grab something to eat. You guys look like you haven't slept in days." Karly chuckled and joined him at the table, though she picked at her food, still lost in thought.

Eli grabbed a plate and sat beside Nathan, though he wasn't really hungry. His mind was still reeling from everything that had happened.

For a few minutes, they ate in silence, the normalcy of the breakfast routine grounding them after the chaos of the last night. The other students were completely unaware of what they had been through, and for a moment, it felt like they were keeping a secret from the rest of the world.

They sat in silence for a few minutes until Karly spoke, "I have a strange feeling still like it isn't over. I'm not sure how to explain it, but it just seems, odd." "I feel it too weirdly enough," Eli replied, as they looked at Nathan.

Nathan groaned, leaning back in his chair. "Come on, you guys. We returned the treasure, passed all the trials, and survived. What else could there be?" Karly glanced down at the table, her fingers absently tracing patterns in the condensation from her glass. "I don't know. But it feels like something's still, I don't know."

The rest of the Nile cruise was uneventful and boring as Mr. Duncan droned about the sand dunes and the Nile. Nathan, Karly and Eli were all quite tired; Nathan and Karly dozed off in a hammock whilst Eli fought sleep, sitting on a wooden box against the edge of the boat. When the boat finally docked, the students were gathered and herded toward the buses waiting to take them to the airport.

The group chatter picked up again, excitement brewing about heading back home, but Eli's mind was elsewhere.

As he stared out the window of the bus, watching the Cairo skyline fade into the distance, a growing pit formed in his stomach.

Karly was sitting beside him, lost in her own thoughts, occasionally glancing toward Nathan, who had managed to fall asleep in the back seat. Eli didn't know what to say. The further they got from the desert and the tomb, the more he hoped Karly was wrong—that the feeling of something being unfinished was just nerves. They had survived the gods, hadn't they?

But as they neared the airport, the familiar buzzing of civilization pulled them from their thoughts. The airport was bustling with travellers from all over the world, the normality of it all weird after what they'd been through.

The group went through check-in without much fuss, and the students were eager to board their flight home. Eli, Karly, and Nathan stuck together, carrying only the essentials as they lined up for security. The process was uneventful, and soon, they were boarding the plane, ready for the long journey back.

Eli found his seat, sinking into the cushion with a sigh of relief. For the first time since they left the tomb, he felt like maybe, just maybe, they were in the clear. Karly sat beside him, still quiet, and very tired. Nathan, who had been unusually quiet since leaving the river, plopped down in his seat across the aisle.

The plane took off smoothly, and soon the familiar hum of the engines filled the cabin. Most of the students had already dozed off, including Karly, who had curled up in her seat, her face finally relaxed after the adventure of the past few days. Eli gazed out the window, watching as the desert below gave way to endless clouds.

Nathan shifted in his seat, feeling something hard pressing against his back. He reached into the side pocket of his bag, fingers brushing against something small and smooth. His breath caught in his throat as he pulled out a familiar object, a scarab amulet, its surface dark and gleaming in the dim cabin light. His eyes widened in disbelief as he stared at the amulet. It must have slipped into his bag back at the tomb. A chill ran down his spine, but he quickly stuffed it back into the pocket, glancing around to make sure no one had seen it.

Nathan glanced over at Eli and Karly, both fast

asleep.

As the plane soared higher, Nathan leaned back in his seat, trying to calm the uneasy feeling gnawing at him. But deep down, he knew that the curse wasn't over. Not yet.

# The End